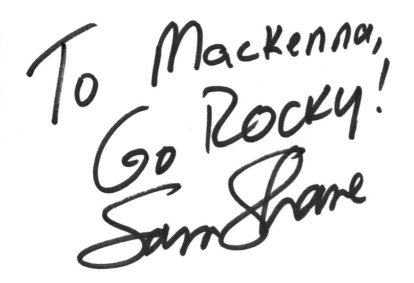

To Mackenna,
Go Rocky!
Sam Shane

Printed in the United States of America
Designed by Dan Marso
First Edition
ISBN: 978-0-9748922-1-4

For information on special discounts for bulk purchases and Rocky The Mudhen merchandise, please contact Rabbit Ears Press & Co., P.O. Box 1952, Davis, CA 95617 or visit our Web site at http://www.rockythemudhen.com

Today's Starting

Rocky
The Rookie
Miesville Mudhens

Hirwigo
Slugging Sensation
Miesville Mudhens

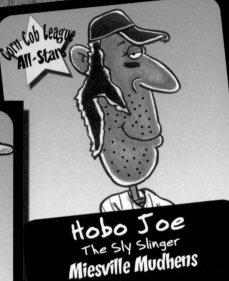

Hobo Joe
The Sly Slinger
Miesville Mudhens

Maggie Megapipes
Radio Announcer
HOGG Radio

Sir Winthrop
The Outhouse Mouse
Miesville Mudhens

The Bomber
Fearsome Slugger
Red Wing Aces

Line-up

Skipper
Gutsy Manager
Miesville Mudhens

Hairball
Hotdoggin' Outfielder
Miesville Mudhens

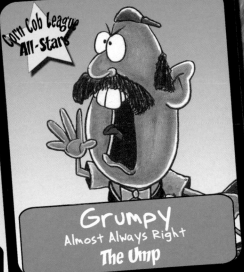

Grumpy
Almost Always Right
The Ump

Bunyan
The Human Toolbox
Grounds Crew

Diego
Rugged Catcher
Miesville Mudhens

Hammer
Keepin' It Real
Grounds Crew

When you see a hot dog next to a word....

... just look down at the bottom of the page and we'll tell you what it means.

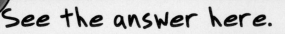

See the answer here.

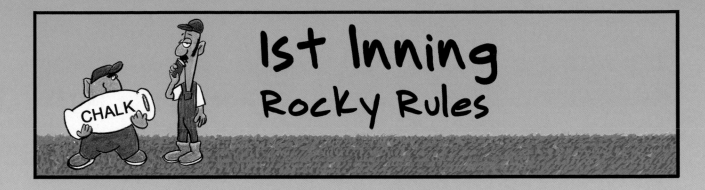

1st Inning
Rocky Rules

Now Rocky was a star.

As Rocky walked to the plate Hirwigo puffed up and unloaded a chest bump on Rocky and said,

"Hit a  rod Rocky!"

Rod = A hard hit ball.

The Dukes' pitcher wound up and threw a hanger. Rocky swung.

CRACK!

He crushed a frozen rope in the gap.

CRACK!

Hanger = A curveball that doesn't break.
Frozen Rope = A hard hit line drive.
Gap = The space between outfielders.

The next batter, Hairball, the sleek and sneaky Mudhens' outfielder, had a little surprise up his sleeve. He dropped down a nifty little bunt. A delicate dandy that dribbled to a dead stop.

Rocky zipped down the third base line and slid smoothly across home plate.

"SAFE!" screamed Grumpy the Ump.

"Mudhens win!" yelled Maggie.

The fans went wild.

2nd Inning
Read All About It!

Everyone was buzzing about Rocky. He was hitting pills at the plate, snagging fly balls in the outfield and swiping bases at eye-popping speed. Happy fans loved to read about it in the newspaper.

Rocky Is The New Fan Favorite!

Mudhens Win!
Rocky Stars In Win.
Details on page 6.

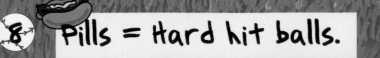

Pills = Hard hit balls.

3rd Inning
Like a Rock Star

When the Jordan Brewers rolled into town the Mudhens' luck changed. The mighty Mudhens were not so mighty. The Brewers lit up Hobo Joe, the Mudhens' crafty pitcher, like a Christmas tree. As the game wore on the Brewers were crushing the Mudhens 9 to 1.

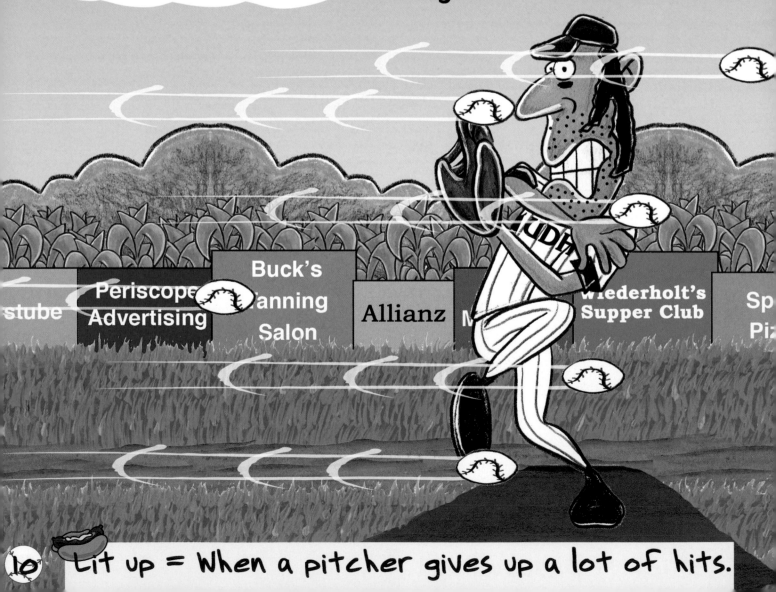

Lit up = When a pitcher gives up a lot of hits.

Hobo Joe thumbed a deuce. The Brewers' hitter lifted a bleeder to center field. Rocky raced in, dove and snagged a spectacular catch.
But in the end the Mudhens lost 10 to 2.

Thumbed = Tossed or thrown slowly.

Deuce = Curveball.

Bleeder = A weakly hit ball.

Afterwards, with cameras and reporters all around Rocky, Maggie Megapipes asked, "Hey Rocky how do you feel about losing so badly? It wasn't even close."
"It's no big deal," said Rocky. "I got my knocks, I stole a base and I made an awesome catch in the outfield. I played a great game. That's all that matters."

Knocks = Base hits.

Rocky thought he was more important than the team. "I don't need to practice, I'm the best player in the Corn Cob League," thought Rocky.

He stopped going to B.P. and shagging fly balls. Instead he sat in the dugout eating hot dogs and telling jokes to reporters.

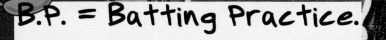

B.P. = Batting Practice.

13

Hairball, Skipper, Hirwigo and Hobo Joe were in a state of shock. They couldn't believe what they just heard. Rocky was not just a star. Now he was a selfish star.
"We've lost five games in a row and all Rocky cares about is himself," said Skipper.

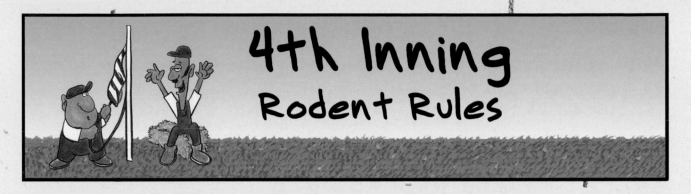

4th Inning
Rodent Rules

The Mudhens were ice cold when the Arlington A's came calling.

Skipper sat in the dugout and tried to figure out how to turn around his troubled team.

When suddenly out swung a mouse on a rope dangling from the corner of the dugout!

"Good Day Skip," said the mouse.

"Sir Winthrop, good to see you again!" said Skipper.

Sir Winthrop The Outhouse Mouse was a wise little critter that lived in the outhouse next to the dugout. Sir Winthrop was Skipper's secret friend who, now and then, paid a visit to the dugout to give Skipper a few tidbits of advice.

"Skip you don't look like you're having much fun," said Sir Winthrop.

"I'm not, we're in the tank and Rocky is out of control."

"Yeah, I noticed. The kid's got a swellin' melon."

"A what?"

"A swellin' melon, you know, a big head, Rocky's too cool to care."

"What should I do, Sir Winthrop?"

"Don't worry about the kid. Trust me he's livin' in a tree right now. He'll come back down to earth eventually. Skip, you need to shake it up. Go find a new player who cares more about the team than himself."

"Well, alrighty then," said Skipper. "Thanks Sir Winthrop."

Livin' in a tree = A player who plays better than he usually plays.

18

5th Inning
New Kid in Town

"Boys I want you to meet Diego, our new catcher," said Skipper.
"Welcome to the club!"

Sure enough Diego was a big hit! He hit pills. He had a hose for an arm and he ran like a deer. Diego blasted booming dingers and soon the Mudhens were winning and their fans were cheering.

"Diego saves the day!" announced Maggie Megapipes.

Hose = Strong Arm.

Dingers = Home Runs.

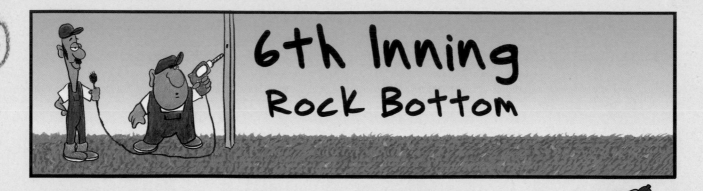

6th Inning
Rock Bottom

As Diego soared Rocky sank. He was in a slump to beat all slumps. He struck out and dropped pop ups. He couldn't hit a beach ball. He couldn't catch a cold if he tried. No more ropes. No more steals. No more reporters. No more cameras.

Rocky hit rock bottom.

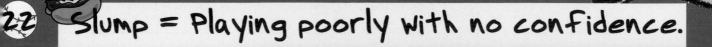

Slump = Playing poorly with no confidence.

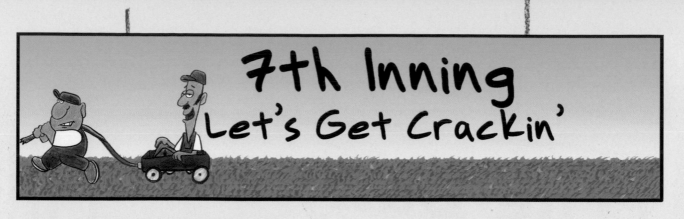

Skipper looked over to see Sir Winthrop back in the dugout.

"Seems like Diego's the real deal and Rocky has checked out."

"You got that right, Sir Winthrop," said Skipper.

"You know Skip, Rocky's a good kid. Maybe you just need to talk to him."

Alrighty then, thanks Sir Winthrop."

Checked out = Not competing hard.

"Not a problem Skip. I gotta run - gotta get to the store to pick up some air fresheners for the outhouse."

Skipper slid down the bench next to Rocky. "Listen, you're a great player and you love the game. You just got caught up in all the excitement. You forgot one basic rule Rocky - no one player is more important than the team. It's time to get to work. I want you back here at the park early tomorrow taking B.P. and shagging fly balls," said Skipper.

That's what Rocky did. Day after day he practiced and soon he realized if he wanted to be a great player, he had to work hard.

SWAAACK!!

8th Inning
Bomber's Back

"The red hot Red Wing Aces and The Bomber have invaded Miesville today for a huge tilt, and it's been a dandy," said Maggie Megapipes. "It looks like Rocky's hard work has paid off. He's gone yard twice and has two stolen bases."

Tilt = Game.

Gone Yard = Home run.

By the 9th inning the Mudhens led 3 to 2.
Hobo Joe gazed at home plate with two outs
and nobody on.
There stood The Bomber.
A mountain of a
man. Forearms
cut like steel.
A neck the
size of a
tree trunk.

Hobo Joe wound up and threw an 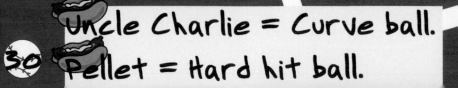Uncle Charlie.
The Bomber swung.

CRACK!

A pellet shot off his bat.

CRACK!

Uncle Charlie = Curve ball.
Pellet = Hard hit ball.

Rocky turned and darted to the fence.
The ball hit the wall and dropped like
a lead balloon.

The Bomber galloped around second base... and he KEPT GOING! The Bomber tried to stretch a double into a home run!

Rocky picked up the ball and uncorked a strike into the mitt of Diego who was waiting at home plate. Diego turned...

33

The Bomber and Diego
collided in a cloud of Dust!

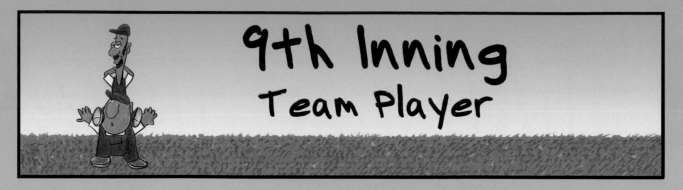

9th Inning
Team Player

After the game Maggie interviewed Rocky. "Hey Rocky, you hit two home runs, you stole a base and you threw out The Bomber at home plate. You were awesome! How does it feel?"

"Thanks Maggie, I'm happy with how I played today. But do you know what matters? Do you know what's really important?"

"We won," Rocky smiled. "What we do as a team is always more important than what I do as a player."

On that day Rocky and the Mudhens were winners.

The Authors

Dan Marso
Age 10 (Now 42)

Sam Shane
Age 7 (Now 43)

Our vision for Rocky The Mudhen when we began this journey in 2002 was to create an educational and entertaining series filled with fun characters and a lively, meaningful message.

Illustrator Dan Marso, a self-taught cartoonist, created a unique and genuine look and feel to our books thanks to his many days of doodling in elementary classrooms and countless summer days on the baseball fields in his hometown of Mankato, Minnesota.

Author Sam Shane developed a dialogue inspired by the real-life characters who crossed his path throughout his amateur baseball career which began in his hometown of Hastings, Minnesota.

The reaction to Rocky The Mudhen from kids and parents has far exceeded our expectations. In four years we've released two books, two series of cartoons (seen on Major League and Minor League baseball stadium scoreboards) and a new Rocky The Mudhen song.

We're grateful for the support of all Rocky The Mudhen fans and we hope you enjoy this latest addition.

Special Thanks:

John "Bon" Amann, Charlie Callahan, Tom Nguyen, Dave Kamish, Rich Olson, Patrick Klinger, Deb Belinsky.